Mistaken Heart

Linda Wagner

Copyright

Copyright © 2021, 2024. Linda Wagner. All rights reserved. Third edition.

The characters and events portrayed in this book are fictitious. Any similarity to actual people, living or dead, is coincidental and not intended by the author.

No part of this book may be reproduced, stored in a retrieval system, or transmitted in any form or by any means, electronic, mechanical, photocopying, recording, or otherwise, without express written permission of the publisher.

Description

In this blend of JAFF and dark paranormal fiction, young Miss Elizabeth Bennet is uprooted to London to live with the Gardiner family after her older brother, James, sells Longbourn. Following a year of mourning, Elizabeth visits her cousins, Mr. William Collins and Mrs. Charlotte Collins.

During her stay at Hunsford parsonage, Mr. Fitzwilliam Darcy and Colonel Richard Fitzwilliam arrive at Rosings Park, the residence of their aunt, Lady Catherine de Bourgh. Both gentlemen are quickly captivated by Elizabeth's charm, finding her sweet, witty, and delightfully innocent. Despite his reserved demeanor, Darcy's heart is immediately engaged. His resolve to make her his wife ignites a fierce rivalry with the more affable Colonel Fitzwilliam, a conflict threatening to tear their friendship asunder.

Elizabeth becomes infatuated with the charismatic Colonel Fitzwilliam, dismissing Darcy's quiet reserve as dislike. However, during a stroll on a crisp September day, a startling revelation shatters her romantic illusions and exposes the dark reality of dragons.

Table of Contents

Dedication

*The wonderful world Jane Austen created will always inspire my soul.
Thank you, Miss Austen, for penning those beautiful novels.
Thanks to my husband, who has listened to my strange imaginings and
always laughed at the right places over the years. He is the most wonderful
man I've ever known.*

Chapter 1

Wednesday: Kent - September 27, 1809

The fragrance of late summer blooms filled the air as Colonel Fitzwilliam joined Miss Elizabeth Bennet as she walked the paths around Rosings Park, his aunt's sprawling estate. Sunlight highlighted Lizzy's deep auburn curls, displayed charmingly by her bonnet, accentuating the young lady's beauty.

Colonel Fitzwilliam beamed at her, eyes dancing with delight. "Miss Bennet, this is a fortunate encounter. I have wonderful news." He took her arm and linked it with his before leading her down the path toward the vicarage.

"What news has made you so happy, Colonel Fitzwilliam?" she asked, gazing at him with adoring eyes. He was tall, handsome, and charming, meeting her almost daily on her walks and flattering her with his attention.

"I'm the happiest of men! Cousin Anne has agreed to marry me. I'll give up my commission, live a life befitting my station, and have enough wealth to afford everything a man of my consequence desires. We'll be very happy." Richard prattled on until Elizabeth withdrew her hand from his arm. Surprised and hurt by the revelation, Elizabeth was overcome by sadness and betrayal, silent tears running down her cheeks.

"No need for tears, my dear. After the nuptials, there will be a place for you as my mistress. A comfortable home, with servants, conveniently close to me," he mentioned casually, his words slicing through her heart like a dagger.

Shock transformed into fury, and Elizabeth's reserve shattered. In a surge of emotion, she slapped him hard across the cheek. Without a word, she fled down the path, her feet crushing fallen flower petals, leaving behind a disconcerted Colonel Fitzwilliam, his cheek stinging.

Reaching the safety of the vicarage, Elizabeth, a tear-soaked, hysterical mess, managed to stammer out the dreadful tale to Mrs. Collins. Her words, distorted by sobs, spilled forth incoherently as she clung to her friend. Charlotte, though trying to provide comfort, found herself helpless in the face of Elizabeth's overwhelming grief. The violent sobbing continued until exhaustion claimed Elizabeth, and she succumbed to a fitful sleep on the parlor couch.

A profoundly concerned Charlotte, her heart racing, urgently sought her husband in his study. A nervous, determined knock preceded her entrance, and she found her husband deeply engrossed in his papers. He sat at his desk, pen in hand, diligently writing a sermon.

Charlotte anxiously wrung her hands together as her words spilled out in a rush. "William, you must go to Rosings Park. Colonel Fitzwilliam insulted Lizzy. She cried herself to sleep on the couch. I'm not sure what he said, but it was terrible. It would be best if you found out what happened. We may need to send her back to London. There might be a scandal if we keep her here."

Mr. Collins looked up from his sermon, placed the pen down, and listened to his wife. Her words made little sense, but it was clear that Colonel Fitzwilliam had somehow insulted his young cousin. There was only one thing to do. Rising from his chair, he straightened the papers on his desk before approaching his wife. He took her hand, raised it to his lips, and kissed it reassuringly.

"Do not worry, my dear. I'm sure it is a small misunderstanding. I'll go to the manor and speak with the colonel. Everything will be fine. You look after Elizabeth." He dropped her hand and left the room with purposeful strides, the door closing behind him, leaving an anxious Charlotte to deal with a heartbroken Elizabeth.

Chapter 2

<u>Confrontation at Rosings</u>

When Mr. Collins arrived at Rosings, slightly out of breath, the butler escorted him to the library, where Mr. Darcy and Colonel Fitzwilliam were loudly arguing. The quarreling ceased abruptly upon his entrance. Darcy greeted Mr. Collins with a slight bow and a cold expression.

"What brings you to Rosings today, Mr. Collins? Is anything amiss?" Darcy's voice was calm and polite, but his eyes betrayed a hint of impatience.

"Yes, indeed, sir. My young cousin, Elizabeth, is hysterical," replied the vicar, slicing the air with an agitated hand. Mr. Collins turned an accusing gaze toward a smirking Colonel Fitzwilliam. "What have you done to cause Elizabeth's distress, sir? The little my wife could understand from her incoherent ramblings implied you insulted her in the basest manner. You have wounded her pride and her feelings most grievously."

The colonel laughed, then mockingly repeated his conversation with Elizabeth, adding a lewd gesture. He barely finished recounting the story when the handprint on his cheek, left by Elizabeth's slap, was joined by the imprint of Darcy's fist to his jaw and another to his eye. The parson stood shaking in shock as he witnessed the violence between the gentlemen.

"How dare you!" Darcy thundered, his eyes blazing with fury. Storming around the room, he pointed a finger at his cousin and spat out, "How dare you act in such a manner with a gentleman's daughter? A young lady just out of mourning who has no experience with men or flirtation? The girl just turned eighteen nine days ago! You had a slice of the birthday cake, you clodpate. Shame on you, Richard, for speaking to her in such a manner. You insulted her and her family." His voice was low and fierce, and his face was red with anger.

Clutching his bruised face, Colonel Fitzwilliam glared at Darcy but said nothing, knowing he had crossed a line. Mr. Collins, still trembling, stepped back, unsure of how to proceed in the tense silence that followed.

An irritated mutter spewed from the colonel's mouth. "An offer of protection from an earl's son is an insult for a penniless girl? Absurd. I would treat her well. She's a lively little..." Any further commentary was cut off when Darcy delivered a crushing blow to his jaw that knocked him into oblivion. Richard fell to the floor with a thud and lay there motionless. Mr. Collins was horrified by the additional display of violence.

Darcy shook his head as if to clear it and turned to the vicar. "Hopefully, my cousin will be unconscious for a few minutes. Mr. Collins, please accept my apologies for the insult to your young cousin. Richard and I are both at fault for visiting the parsonage daily. I saw her regard for my cousin and hoped it was a passing infatuation. I plan to make her my wife. The area residents probably expect an engagement to be announced." He spoke with sincerity and regret, his eyes softening as he mentioned Elizabeth.

Mr. Collins, stunned by Darcy's declaration, went to a chair and sat.

"You plan to marry Lizzy? She will be surprised, indeed. You never showed your interest to her. My wife and I suspected it and tried to tell her of your affection. She didn't believe us. Colonel Fitzwilliam's attentions clouded her eyes." Mr. Collins rubbed his face with both hands, trying to calm himself.

"Elizabeth cried herself to sleep after an hour of hysterical sobbing. We are unsure if the tears are disappointment or anger at being insulted by someone she considered a friend. Plus, my wife is distraught and claims the girl should return to London, where her remaining family can comfort her. She will face ruination if she remains here; what am I to tell the girl?" sputtered Collins. The vicar's rage caused his voice to shake. He feared for Elizabeth's reputation and happiness.

The situation was intolerable. Darcy glared at Richard, who was still lying on the floor. He contemplated punching Richard again to blacken his other eye.

His dragon, Zander, stopped him. The being that could control his every action. It was his inescapable fate to host a dragon. He felt the dragon's power surge within him, and he struggled to maintain his demeanor. The unseen voice that ruled him spoke.

Zander proclaimed, "He will be punished for this transgression. Every one of Elizabeth's tears will be noted. Richard will feel her pain tenfold. I sent for Tor, one of my inquisitors, to meet us in London for the reckoning. I'm informing our people to prepare for departure in the morning. Take care of the girl. She hasn't been told of her heritage."

Darcy replied, "What?!? How is this possible? She will be overwhelmed by the joining."

Zander instructed, "She will survive. Go to the vicarage now. Our people will take care of everything here."

Darcy turned to Mr. Collins, "We'll take Elizabeth to London tomorrow morning. Richard and I will escort the carriage on horseback and have a maid sit with her inside. Your wife must join them. I will come with you now and speak to her." He went to the door, opened it, and left the library with Mr. Collins following. Neither gave the prone body on the floor a glance.

Chapter 3

Elizabeth lay on the couch, curled into a ball; her sleeping form filled Darcy with renewed anger at his cousin. Her tear-stained cheeks were drained of color, and her gasping breaths convinced Darcy that the girl still suffered from Richard's news and indecent proposal. He was outraged that nobody had covered her body or put her to bed. He leaned down, gathered her into his arms, and headed up the stairs, calling for Charlotte to direct him to Elizabeth's room.

After placing her in bed and gently covering her, Darcy pulled a chair over to its side and sat down. He looked at Charlotte and her husband. "Don't bother protesting. I will stay with her. A cup of coffee or tea would be welcome while I wait for her to wake up. Consider her my fiancé. Her uncle will give his consent. My cousin has forced my hand by his reprehensible behavior. I wanted her to know me better."

He looked at the couple and sighed. Mr. and Mrs. Collins stood in the doorway wearing identical expressions of dismay. He could not say anything to improve the situation, but he tried to curb his anger.

"Have the servants pack her trunks. I won't mind their presence." He turned his attention back to the sleeping girl. She moved restlessly under the covers as Mrs. Collins, with the soft rustle of skirts, left to instruct the servants. Seconds later, Mr. Collins' heavy footsteps descended the stairs.

Darcy gave a nod of thanks when a servant delivered a tea tray and placed it on the nightstand. He poured himself a cup of tea. He watched Elizabeth sleep as he sipped the tea. Sleep was not giving her the respite she needed. She twisted, turned, and whimpered. He surmised that her dreams were not comforting.

Two hours later, Elizabeth woke up crying in distress. It took her a few seconds to recognize her room, and the people packing her trunks looked at her surreptitiously. Hovering by the bed, Charlotte grasped her hand, capturing her attention. "Easy, Lizzy. Mr. Darcy carried you up when he arrived and found you lying on the sofa. We've all been here waiting for you to wake up. Do you feel any better?" she asked.

Elizabeth's searching gaze fell upon Darcy, seated in a chair beside the bed, silently watching the hurried movements of servants packing her trunks. Overwhelmed by confusion, she cried out in distress, her voice a tremulous plea. "What's going on? Why are you all here? Am I in trouble?"

Hearing the tremor in her voice, Darcy responded with immediate reassurance, seeking to address her foremost concern. "No, Elizabeth. You are not in trouble. We are all here because we care about you." His words, laden with sincerity, were calming. "The servants are packing your trunks. You will return to London to stay with the Gardiners tomorrow morning in my carriage with a maid and Mrs. Collins if her husband allows it."

"Why?" she implored. She tried to hold back her tears but lost the battle. "I did not do anything wrong! I want to stay here with Charlotte. I missed her so much." Her tears, now accompanied by heart-wrenching sobs, filled the room.

Unable to witness her anguish from a distance, Darcy rose from his chair and reached for Elizabeth, gently pulling her from the bed and settling her on his lap. Enveloping her in a protective embrace, he ran a soothing hand up and down her trembling back, an attempt to offer solace amid the storm of emotions.

In a tender whisper, Darcy spoke directly to her, his words providing little comfort. "We go to London tomorrow to finalize our formal engagement with your Uncle Gardiner. Richard and I spent more time with you than proper. I planned to get to know you better before asking for your hand. Richard's behavior today and your reaction have made our immediate engagement necessary. Do you understand what I'm saying to you, Elizabeth?"

He rested his chin on top of her head as she continued to cry. She shook her head in denial; questions swirled in her mind like a tempest. How could she marry this enigmatic man? Always quiet, hardly speaking a word to her, she thought he disliked her. His eyes followed her with a darkness she found indecipherable. She had perceived a certain aloofness in his demeanor, an inscrutable darkness in his gaze. How could he want to marry her? Why was he holding her? Why did his touch give her comfort, an unexpected solace, a refuge in the storm of her emotions? What was happening to her? Her distress grew, rendering her immobile, and she wept bitter tears of uncertainty.

In the embrace of his arms, she eventually succumbed to exhaustion, falling into a fitful slumber. Darcy's gaze shifted to Charlotte, meeting her disapproving glare with restrained anger.

"You know her heritage. You and your husband have not been chosen. It is both a pleasure and a curse for the host. There is nothing to be done except for the will of my dragon. It is his will that demands her removal from your home. I don't care for appearances at this point, Mrs. Collins. She will marry me as soon as I get the license in London. Being angry at me is a waste of time. I am not the person who blatantly flirted with her in your presence and then insulted her and your family while she walked the grounds alone. It is not your dragon's mate that must join with the girl before knowing her better."

Charlotte, recognizing the futility of anger directed at Darcy, rose from her seat and left the room. He was correct. As a married woman and chaperone, her responsibility was to curb the colonel's behavior. Darcy loved the girl; listening to each word the girl spoke, his eyes followed Lizzy's every move.

Conversations with her husband often centered around their shared concern for Lizzy's future and Darcy's growing interest during visits. As a confidante and friend, Charlotte had diligently shared her views with Lizzy. She tried to warn Lizzy that Colonel Fitzwilliam had a reputation as a notorious flirt, and Darcy appeared to have a serious interest. Mr. Collins tried to caution his cousin to guard her heart. Yet, regrettably, neither had explicitly asked the colonel to exercise restraint.

When the servants left the room, Darcy placed Elizabeth back on the bed, then closed and latched the door, peeling off most of his garments. Standing beside the bed wearing his shirt and breeches, he gazed upon Lizzy's beautiful, tear-streaked face. With a deliberate gentleness, he removed all her garments except a delicate chemise. Joining her on the bed, Darcy pulled her into his arms and held her close, driven by an instinctual knowledge of what was needed. Leaning down, he tenderly kissed her neck, a comforting and intimate gesture, before extending his fangs and biting down with determination.

Zander flooded her system with healing venom while Darcy stroked her side gently with a hand, waiting patiently for Kira to enter the girl's body, then claimed her as his mate with a deeper bite and more venom that would inscribe his portrait on her back.

Slowly, the silhouette of a golden dragon in flight took shape under her skin and then rose to the surface luminous. Kira took control of Elizabeth's body and reciprocated the ritual. Her iridescent white dragon took its place on his back. There would be no turning back for Elizabeth and Darcy.

After the ritual, Darcy fell into a deep sleep. He woke at sunrise, dressed himself and his peacefully sleeping mate, and left the room to find a servant who could prepare an early breakfast. The household was stirring, and Mr. and Mrs. Collins patiently awaited him.

Darcy addressed their unspoken concerns. "Don't worry. We are mated in the traditional way of our kind. I have not harmed her. She slept through her joining and the exchange of bites. Will you be traveling with us today, Mrs. Collins? It may help reassure her on the trip."

Mrs. Collins responded in the affirmative. "Yes, Mr. Darcy. I'll go with her in the carriage. I may calm her when she sees Colonel Fitzwilliam riding his horse beside the carriage. I hope to attend the wedding and make some purchases in town. Will you provide transportation for the return trip after the wedding?" Charlotte inquired, her eyes reflecting her concern.

Darcy glanced at Mr. Collins, seeking his approval. "If your husband doesn't mind letting you remain with Elizabeth and the Gardiners for a few days, it will be my honor to have you at the wedding and provide your transportation back home."

A nod of approval came from Mr. Collins, yet his eyes glowed with discontent. His anger at Colonel Fitzwilliam's mistreatment of Elizabeth, a young woman burdened with profound losses, simmered beneath the surface. The vicar found himself astounded by the colonel's total disregard for the feelings of others. At that moment, he harbored a deep and genuine pity for Miss Anne, who was engaged to marry an unfeeling womanizer.

The girl had not expected a joining and reacted badly when she woke to find herself host to Kira and mated to Darcy. Proof of the event was the luminescent golden dragon on her back and the voice in her mind. She had heard stories of people who were dragon hosts but had never thought the stories were true. Why had nobody told her that she was an unclaimed host? Terrified, Lizzy started to scream. Kira immediately took control of Elizabeth's body, and the girl silently got out of bed, finished packing, and ate breakfast.

The carriage arrived, its wheels crunching on the gravel, and Elizabeth and Charlotte began a journey that would redefine Elizabeth's life. Seated beside Elizabeth, Charlotte held her hand tightly, her gaze never leaving the young woman's face. The array of emotions displayed in Elizabeth's countenance and the complete silence evoked a deep concern in Charlotte, a recognition that a dragon was controlling her friend.

Evidently, the Bennets had not enlightened Elizabeth about her true nature. The assumption that the children had been taught about their ability to host the dragon spirits, which ruled the planet, seemed misplaced. Charlotte recognized a gap in Elizabeth's understanding that perhaps the Gardiners had assumed was filled. Not all hosts were chosen as babies; some, like Charlotte and her husband, were never chosen by a dragon.

Chapter 4

Journey to London

Throughout the trip, Kira described Elizabeth's new life as Darcy's wife, emphasizing the unique responsibilities of hosting the dragon queen and being the mate of the dragon king's host.

Kira's voice was soothing as she explained, "Elizabeth, as my host, you will have duties beyond the ordinary. You will marry Darcy, the dragon king's host. Your roles are filled with immense honor and responsibility."

Elizabeth listened intently, her brows furrowed in concentration. "What exactly will be expected of me?" she asked, her words tinged with apprehension.

"The boundaries are clearly defined. Specific activities are forbidden, while others are deemed essential. You must learn these quickly, but you won't be alone. I will be your best friend and confidant in this transformative journey. I'll teach you things as you sleep. You'll be surprised at how much you know."

Elizabeth nervously nodded. "I don't understand why I can't move..."

"I can hear your thoughts. Our joining distresses you. You were about to scream. I'm sorry your heritage wasn't explained to you, but indulging in hysterics and attempting to run away will not be tolerated. Dangerous activities are not allowed. Once you accept the situation, I'll stop controlling your body."

Elizabeth took a deep breath, feeling a bit more at ease. "What if I don't want to be your host. Can't you leave?"

Kira laughed, a tinkling musical roar. "Elizabeth, if I leave, you will die, and Darcy will be upset. We are past the stage where you have a choice. The first part of the bonding ritual is complete. Under draconic law, you are married. Having a marriage ceremony is for the unclaimed and humans."

Lizzy was reeling in shock. "Kira, what will I be expected to do as Darcy's wife?"

"On a personal level, you will perform all the expected wifely duties associated with marriage. Dragon hosts have large sexual appetites." Kira let her words sink into Lizzy's mind before continuing. "You will host and attend numerous social gatherings, including balls, dinners, and teas. These events will be crucial for maintaining social alliances and fulfilling your role as hostess. However, certain gatherings involving the draconic community require discretion and adherence to their customs. Nudity is common in some areas."

Elizabeth interjected, "And my wardrobe? I only have a few practical gowns. How can I host elegant parties in muslin dresses?"

"Indeed. You must wear attire befitting your new status, including silk or velvet gowns suitable for formal events that reflect your elevated position. Special garments or nudity will be required for dragon-related ceremonies and gatherings. We will ensure you have everything you need, and I will help you navigate any unfamiliar customs."

"What about our homes? Where will we be living?"

"You and Darcy will reside primarily at Pemberley, his ancestral home. It will serve as your main residence. It is a vast estate with numerous responsibilities, including managing the household staff and overseeing the estate's affairs. Additionally, you will have a residence in London for the social season and the special quarters for hosting dragons when required. Darcy owns other estates around the world that you may visit," came the reply.

Overwhelmed, Lizzy's questions were a mental whisper. "And visiting others? How often will we be expected to travel?"

"You will frequently visit the noble families of humans, hosts, and dragons to maintain strong relations. These visits can range from a few days to several weeks, depending on the occasion. Traveling will be a significant part of your life, but it will also provide opportunities to strengthen bonds and fulfill your duties as Darcy's wife."

Elizabeth took a deep breath, processing the information. "Thank you, Kira. I'm not sure I can do this."

Kira replied, "Together, we will ensure you excel in your new roles, Elizabeth. You are more capable than you realize, and I am confident you will rise to the occasion splendidly. I will always be available to answer your questions. I'm going to let you rest and begin teaching you about dragons. When you wake, you'll regain control of your body and possess a rudimentary understanding of your species."

Chapter 5

A surprised Mrs. Gardiner welcomed the unexpected party upon their arrival at Gracechurch Street. Following the requisite introductions, Charlotte sought refuge in a guestroom, and Elizabeth retreated to her room to refresh and change. Darcy remained in the parlor with Colonel Fitzwilliam to explain Elizabeth's early return, escorted by two gentlemen.

"Mrs. Gardiner, I'm sorry for this unexpected intrusion into your home. Due to unforeseen circumstances, Miss Bennet needed to return here immediately. Rather than repeat the story multiple times, it may be best if you summon your husband home." Darcy's words were a command, emphasized by a flash of gold in his eyes.

Astounded by the revelation that this man hosted a royal dragon, specifically the king, Mrs. Gardiner called for a servant and sent him to bring her husband home. After leaving the two men in the parlor with a tea tray ordered, she went to assist her niece. Entering the room without knocking, she was surprised to see a golden dragon displayed on Elizabeth's back.

Madeline Gardiner exclaimed, "Bloody hell, Elizabeth! You've been joined with the queen and mated to the king!"

Madeline bowed her head to the queen. Her dragon, Laura, spoke to Kira.

Elizabeth went behind a screen to hide her back from the servants when a maid bearing warm water and towels knocked on the door. Madeline helped her niece wash the road dust from her body, dressed her in a pretty gown, did her hair in a simple style, hugged her, told her she was loved, and led her downstairs to the parlor.

Madeline Gardiner settled on the sofa, her eyes tracking her niece's rapid pacing around the parlor. Elizabeth's unexpected arrival in the company of Fitzwilliam Darcy and Colonel Richard Fitzwilliam stirred a torrent of questions. Mrs. Gardiner cast a measured glance at the two men seated in chairs, sipping tea while exchanging scowls. Colonel Fitzwilliam's bruised and swollen face hinted at a severe disagreement.

Turning her attention back to Elizabeth, Mrs. Gardiner issued a firm directive. "Do sit down, Lizzy. Your uncle will be here soon. He won't appreciate seeing a path worn into the rug from your pacing."

Elizabeth, complying with her aunt's command, sank into the nearest chair. "Aunt, where are Jane and Mary?" she asked.

Mrs. Gardiner paled. She whispered, "They are in Bath with your aunt, Mrs. Phillips. Amelia wanted to visit friends and invited your sisters to accompany her. I'm sorry they aren't here for you."

Lowering her head, Elizabeth covered her face with her hands. The rapid pounding of her heart reflected the mounting fear that there would be no escape from this marriage. Silently, she prayed for her uncle to arrive, hoping he could convince Mr. Darcy to find another bride.

Kira spoke, "Stop whining. It does no good. You are my host now. It is your heritage. There is no going back, only forward. Learn your role and be content. Your uncle is a host and is subject to our rules. You will marry Darcy, and you will be happy. I'm sorry your sisters will miss the ceremony."

Kira's blunt words echoed in Elizabeth's mind, emphasizing the irrevocable nature of her newfound heritage. The dragon within her urged acceptance and forward momentum, dismissing any futile yearning for a past that could not be reclaimed. Elizabeth harbored an unrealistic wish for Kira to cease her incessant, pragmatic reminders, finding the dragon's commentary on everything irritating.

Elizabeth could no longer contain her frustration. She sighed, rubbing her temples. "Must you always be so direct, Kira? I understand my situation, but your constant reminders are overwhelming."

Kira's voice was calm and unwavering in her mind. "I speak bluntly because your new life leaves no room for misunderstandings."

Elizabeth murmured aloud, her voice filled with resigned frustration. "It's just...a lot to take in. I wish things could go back to how they were."

Mistaking the focus of Lizzy's comment, Aunt Madeline replied, her tone soft. "Longing for the past won't change the future, Elizabeth. Embrace your new heritage, and you will find the strength you never knew you had. Mr.Darcy's substantial wealth, power, and social standing make this an advantageous match, regardless of his status as a host."

Elizabeth clenched her hands in her lap, her knuckles white, and thought, "Uncle Gardiner will agree to this marriage without hesitation. His position as a host makes it unavoidable."

"Yes, and it is a match that will secure your future. Darcy's wealth and power will ensure your place in society and offer you protection in this society," Kira reassured her, her voice echoing Elizabeth's thoughts.

Elizabeth grimaced. "Aunt Maddy's counsel is much like yours...pragmatic. I wish for simpler, more human advice."

"Your aunt speaks from a place of experience. She understands the challenges you face. But remember, you are forging your own path. Take her advice, but shape it to suit your own needs," Kira advised, her voice tinged with understanding.

Elizabeth looked at Darcy, her mind a whirlwind of thoughts. "I'll try, Kira. It's just...so much."

"I know, Lizzy. But you are stronger than you realize. Embrace your destiny, and you will thrive," Kira's voice encouraged.

Elizabeth took a deep breath. "Thank you, Kira. I'll do my best."

"That's all I ask," Kira's voice echoed with determination, bolstering Elizabeth's resolve.

As tears silently rolled down Elizabeth's cheeks, Darcy, noting her distress, rose from his chair. Crossing the room, he offered her his handkerchief and a comforting pat on the shoulder.

Elizabeth dried her tears and clasped her hands tightly in her lap. She spoke quietly, not wishing the others to hear. "There's something I need to share with you, Mr. Darcy. A memory that haunts me, one that has shaped so much of my life for the past few years."

Darcy leaned closer, his expression attentive and concerned. "Of course, Elizabeth. You can tell me anything."

Elizabeth took a deep breath, her voice trembling as she began. "It's about the carriage accident. The day I lost my parents and my two youngest sisters, Kitty and Lydia."

Darcy reached out, taking her hand in his and gently squeezing it. "I'm so sorry, Elizabeth. I can't imagine how difficult that must have been for you."

Elizabeth drew strength from his comforting words. "They were coming home from a visit to Meryton, and Papa promised to buy me a surprise. I was watching the road from my window. The horses turned into the driveway, and one hit the gate with his shoulder. He slammed into the other horse, screaming in pain. The driver lost control, jumped from his seat, and rolled away in the grass. The horses were screaming and thrashing, and then the carriage overturned..."

She paused, her eyes filling with tears. "My parents and youngest sisters were thrown around inside the carriage as it rolled over. The horses were on the ground. The head groom shot the horses while I watched the staff pull my family from the wreckage. I tried to run outside when I could move, but my brother caught me and pushed me back into the house. My parents and sisters died on the driveway. It was horrific."

Darcy's grip tightened around her hand. "Elizabeth, I had no idea."

Elizabeth nodded, her voice barely above a whisper. "Longbourn passed to my brother, James. He had no desire to manage the estate, so he sold it. Half of the proceeds were invested, and the rest was used to buy a shipping company. James found fulfillment and success in that venture."

Darcy listened intently, his eyes never leaving hers. "And what happened to you and your sisters?"

"James sent us to live with the Gardiners, our official guardians. Jane, Mary, and I have been with them ever since. James provides for us, ensuring we have funds for our upkeep and modest dowries," Elizabeth explained, her voice steadying. "Jane is twenty now, I am eighteen, and Mary is sixteen."

Darcy understood her loss. His parents were dead, too. He murmured, "You've been through so much, Lizzy. It's hard to lose the people you love."

Elizabeth looked down, her emotions swirling. "Sometimes, I still see it all in my mind. The accident, the chaos, their bodies. And now, I find myself on the precipice of a marriage I never anticipated."

Darcy reached out, gently lifting her chin so their eyes met. "Elizabeth, I promise you this: I will do everything possible to ensure you are happy and safe."

Elizabeth's eyes softened. "Thank you, Mr. Darcy. Your words mean more to me than you can know."

Darcy leaned in, his voice filled with sincerity. "We will build a future together where you can find peace and joy again. You are not alone, Elizabeth."

Elizabeth felt a warmth spread through her chest, the haunting memories momentarily pushed aside by the promise of a new beginning. "I believe you. With you by my side, life will be different."

Darcy smiled, his eyes filled with love and determination. "Together, we will create a life filled with happiness. I swear it."

Lizzy turned her head away to peer around the room with unseeing eyes. Darcy said nothing; he wanted to give the girl a chance to finish reflecting on her memories.

A few moments later, he heard a raucous laugh from across the room. His attention shifted to his cousin. Mrs. Gardiner was kindly offering Richard a cup of tea. Darcy regarded his cousin with disgust as the man tried to flirt with the unreceptive woman.

Leaning down, Darcy whispered to Elizabeth, his gently formed words intended to cut through her sorrow. "Look at him. Is that how an engaged man behaves if he cares for his betrothed?"

Elizabeth reluctantly gazed at the colonel, seeing him clearly for the first time. Colonel Fitzwilliam had visited the parsonage daily for three weeks, often accompanied by Darcy. He had joked with her, told her stories, complimented her excessively, and walked with her in the garden. She had taken his attention to heart. The young men in Meryton never paid attention to her. Unaccustomed to the company of men, having been in mourning after her parents died, Elizabeth had misconstrued the colonel's intentions; she had mistaken his attention for courtship.

Why had nobody explained the complexities of men to her? Now, seeing the shallowness of his behavior, she realized her misconception and looked away in disillusionment. How could Colonel Fitzwilliam, engaged to another woman, shamelessly attempt to flirt with her aunt despite the visible signs of a black eye and purple bruises? His breach of proper conduct underscored her misunderstanding of his character and intentions.

Kira's laughter echoed in Elizabeth's thoughts as the dragon dismissed Colonel Fitzwilliam with a damning assessment. "He is a selfish rake," Kira declared. "Colonel Fitzwilliam marries Miss Anne for her possessions and sees nothing wrong in flirting with any woman who crosses his path. It is a game a particular type of man plays with willing women to pass the time. Unfortunately, he did not care that you were inexperienced with such games. Darcy played no games. He sat quietly, watching, and hoped you would notice his interest and grace him with your conversation now and then."

Elizabeth lifted her eyes to meet Darcy's penetrating gray gaze, finding his features etched with concern. In a whisper, trying to understand, she said, "I begin to see. Does he not care for me at all?"

Darcy whispered in reply, "He does not love you. He would gladly use your body to pleasure himself. A dragon spirit has not chosen him. He has no inner companion to guide his behavior, and his mind takes him down selfish paths. Cousin Anne will do her best to show him a better way to live if he survives Tor's punishment for what he has done to you. He has been informed of your status as my mate and cannot approach you. Zander will incinerate him if he attempts to harm you in any way."

"Did you do the damage to his face?" she asked.

A smile and a nod were her answer. "Zander kept me from doing more. We leave it to the grand inquisitor to show Richard the joys of hellfire," replied Darcy.

Lifting her chin gently with a finger, Darcy gazed into her emerald eyes and whispered, "You will learn what it feels like to be ardently loved soon. When sharing that love, a dragon mate has endless passion and unimaginable stamina and endurance." Dragon fire glinted in Darcy's eyes as he spoke, eliciting a shiver from Elizabeth in response to his touch and words. Sensing her reaction, Darcy smiled.

A commotion at the front door announced the arrival of Edward Gardiner, host to Tyre, a splendid blue dragon. His entrance drew a relieved glance from his wife, who had risen in response. With a composed demeanor, Mrs. Gardiner introduced the two gentlemen to her husband, explaining that they had escorted the Darcy carriage, carrying a maid, Elizabeth, and Charlotte Collins from Hunsford. She added, "Mr. Darcy has promised to explain why everyone is here. We waited for you to arrive so the story didn't need to be repeated."

Darcy began to speak with polite regret, "Please forgive our unannounced visit. I hope you'll accept my apology for inconveniencing you and your family."

"Think nothing of it. Please get to the events that bring you here," Gardiner stated firmly.

"It's not complicated, Mr. Gardiner. Colonel Fitzwilliam and I were visiting our aunt, Lady Catherine, at Rosings Park, near Hunsford vicarage. Our aunt invited the Collins family and their guest to dine with us shortly after we arrived. Lady Catherine, her daughter Miss Anne, and her companion Mrs. Jenkinson have various habits that make spending time with them stressful. The invitation proved fortuitous because Miss Elizabeth can play the pianoforte and sing like an angel." He smiled kindly at Elizabeth when he mentioned her voice.

"We seized every opportunity to escape the boredom of Rosings and visit with the pleasant company at the vicarage. We went there more often than proper for casual acquaintances. My cousin has a charming personality and a tendency to flirt. I am reticent and tend to observe the intricacies of social interactions."

A barely stifled chuckle emanated from the opposite chair. Darcy gave his cousin a dark look to remind him to keep quiet. "You can see my cousin wants to speak. Most likely, he'd make a joke about my lack of social skills. Unfortunately, his lack of sense has brought us to your home today."

Darcy turned toward Mr. Gardiner, whose expression was growing increasingly grim. He continued, "After Elizabeth turned eighteen, I spoke to Richard and informed him that I planned to court and marry her. I asked him to stop flirting with her. Instead of heeding my request, Colonel Fitzwilliam increased his attention." Both men turned stern, disapproving eyes toward Richard, who responded with a nonchalant shrug.

"My cousin joined Elizabeth while she walked through the park yesterday morning. Richard told her he had asked our cousin, Anne, to marry him. He explained that he was engaged, looking forward to marriage, and anticipating his ability to take Elizabeth to bed as his mistress. Surprised at his engagement and outraged at his indecent proposition, she slapped him across the face, leaving a red handprint visible to all, before fleeing to the vicarage. She arrived home weeping from his callous treatment and insult."

Darcy's words hung in the air; he paused, his gaze fixed on Mr. Gardiner, who, in response, forcefully pulled Richard from the chair and delivered a powerful left hook to his other eye. Richard crumpled to the floor, unconscious, as the room resonated with the impact.

Gardiner spoke through clenched teeth, "If he has half a brain, he will stay down. I may kill him if he gets up."

Darcy agreed with the statement with a slight nod before continuing, "Mr. Collins arrived as I questioned Richard about the handprint on his face. Collins launched into a story of insults and tears. Richard elucidated the tale with its reprehensible details. His words enraged me enough to strike him before my dragon stopped me from killing a relative. Tor has been called to render justice."

Gardiner showed his acceptance. The inquisitor would judge and enforce the punishment for Colonel Fitzwilliam. Mistreating a female of their species was forbidden.

"Please continue with the events. I can see that Elizabeth is not happy." Gardiner's tone was stern, mirroring the concern etched on his face.

"Mr. Collins and I went back to his home. I clarified that I would marry Elizabeth as soon as we could get your approval and a license. He insisted that the gossip surrounding the visits to the vicarage would ruin Elizabeth's reputation unless she left the area before the morning's events became known to the servants and then the locals."

Darcy paused and took a deliberate sip of his tea, his eyes fixed on the cup as though searching for the right words in its depths. The Gardiners waited patiently for him to continue.

"Elizabeth was still sleeping fitfully on the sofa in the parlor when we arrived, so I carried her to her bed and placed her under the covers with the assistance of Mrs. Collins. We sat by the bedside for two hours while servants packed Elizabeth's trunks. When Elizabeth woke, she was still distraught and started sobbing again. We informed her what had happened at Rosings with Richard and that we would marry after getting your approval."

When Darcy finished speaking, he flashed dragon fire from his eyes toward Mr. Gardiner, who recognized the power and authority this imposing dragon host wielded. As the host of a dragon, he had no choice but to consent to the marriage.

"Last night, Elizabeth was joined with her spirit companion and received and gave the traditional mating bite. Be assured the markings are in place, and my heart is engaged. Elizabeth will be loved and cherished as my wife." Darcy looked at both Gardiners and then down at Elizabeth, whose hand he clasped firmly.

Gardiner nodded his approval of the marriage, observing the subtle exchange between Darcy and Lizzy. As Darcy lightly kissed Lizzy on the head, there was a tenderness in the gesture that conveyed more than words could express. Minutes later, a determined Darcy left the house to secure the marriage license as swiftly as possible.

Once he departed, Elizabeth and Madeline retreated to Lizzy's room for a heart-to-heart conversation. The room was filled with the soft glow of a bedside lamp. Still processing the events, Elizabeth was frightened about the future and confused by the implications of the joining. The revelation of Richard's intentions had left her heartbroken, the insult of his words devastating her tender heart. More than the engagement to Anne de Bourgh, Richard's perception of her as a mere distraction...a toy, stung the most.

Sensing Lizzy's emotional distress, Madeline held her niece in a comforting embrace, her gentle strokes soothing the distressed girl. Lizzy, emotionally drained, lay down on her bed, closing her eyes in an attempt to find solace in sleep. Understanding the need for healing, Kira sent Lizzy into a deep, healing sleep.

The sun shone brightly on a field of lavender flowers. The sight was glorious. Overhead, a bird flew towards a distant mountain. It was golden with feathers that reflected the sunlight. No, not feathers. The bird turned and soared toward her, growing more prominent as it neared. It was a dragon!

The feathers were scales. Scales that were tougher than armor, impervious to harm. Zander stood before her in his glorious eternal form. He rose on his hind legs and spread his wings wide for her inspection. Then he laid his body down and stretched out his front legs. His head rested between them, and his eyes met hers. His golden eyes were full of dragon fire and wisdom.

'Do you like what you see, my love? Come closer. Touch me.'

His words drew her closer. She reached out and touched his golden hide and felt its warmth. She stroked his neck and marveled at its softness.

Lizzy woke with a start, the remnants of an excellent dream lingering in her mind, where she almost soared through the skies, riding a golden dragon. The soft calls of her name from Aunt Madeline and Charlotte gently pulled her back to reality while her aunt shook her shoulder to wake her fully. Reluctantly, Lizzy opened her eyes, the dream's magic still dancing at the edges of her consciousness.

"Get out of bed, Lizzy," her aunt excitedly commanded. "Darcy is in the parlor, and he brought the license and the archbishop with him. Time to get you dressed and married."

"Is Colonel Fitzwilliam still here?" she asked.

"Yes, but while you were sleeping, Mr. Gardiner secured him in a guestroom with two footmen standing guard outside the door. He doesn't deserve to share in the festivities planned for you and Mr. Darcy. Plus, we don't want the children to meet that man," Mrs. Gardiner answered curtly.

An hour later, Elizabeth Bennet became Elizabeth Darcy. Instead of a traditional wedding breakfast, they enjoyed an intimate family supper. Laughter, singing, and dancing echoed through the parlor as the household celebrated the union of the newlyweds.

Tor, the London's Grand Inquisitor, arrived as the family was about to call for a late tea service. With a congratulatory tone, he extended his wishes for the couple's happiness and shared a cup of tea with everyone before broaching Colonel Fitzwilliam's transgressions.

The room was silent as Tor listened to Zander and Kira provide an account of recent events.

The inquisitor turned to Richard and said, "Tell me a true story."

Richard was worried about his fate for the first time since arriving in London. He replied, "I don't understand why everyone is upset with me. I offered Lizzy a carte blanche. She refused."

"You are a pitiful specimen of a man. I need a closer inspection of your mind." The stern words preceded Tor's transformation into a seven-foot-tall lion with blazing eyes that invaded Richard's mind, inspecting Richard's actions and leaving behind a fiery trail of pain that would linger for days.

Elizabeth fainted when Tor transformed into a lion. The ethereal voice, claiming to be the dragon queen, had not prepared her for the visceral shock of witnessing an actual transformation. One moment, Tor looked human; the next, he was a mighty lion, his majestic presence filling the space with a tangible sense of fear. Elizabeth's vision blurred, and darkness claimed her.

When Elizabeth stirred, she found herself lying on the couch in Darcy's embrace, a warm blanket draped over her. Now back in his human form, Tor sat nearby, his expression apologetic.

"I'm sorry, Mrs. Darcy," he said quietly, his voice filled with genuine remorse. "I didn't mean to frighten you."

Elizabeth took a deep breath, trying to steady her racing heart. "It's not your fault, Tor. I just... I wasn't ready for that."

Tor nodded in understanding. Elizabeth's gaze met his, a newfound determination flickering in her eyes. "I'll do my best to adapt. I have to."

Tor smiled, his relief evident. "You will, Mrs. Darcy. I must go." He turned to Darcy. "I wish you happiness. Take care of your bride."

Tor took Richard away to face a month of hard labor during daylight hours and receive instruction on proper conduct each night. The inquisitor's judgment was a sobering reminder that consequences awaited those who strayed from the expected path.

As Elizabeth watched Richard depart, a feeling of relief filled her mind. The comforting weight of the blanket and the reassuring presence of Darcy and her family gave her a spark of hope. With Kira's voice guiding her and Darcy's unwavering love, she was ready to embrace her future.

Chapter 6

Friday: September 29, 1809 - Darcy House

Darcy took his bride to Darcy House, leading her directly into the library. Elizabeth, awed, stood still. The room contained hundreds of books, more than she had ever seen in a private home. The scent of aged leather and paper filled the air, creating an atmosphere of intellectual richness.

"This is amazing," she said. Her eyes roamed the shelves. She began wandering between the stacks, tracing the titles with her fingers.

"Come here, Elizabeth. This book is special." Darcy showed her the first edition of Wordsworth's poems. The leather cover felt cool and smooth under her touch.

"Pull it towards you, and magic happens." Darcy pulled the book forward from the top just enough to tilt it. The bookcase moved away from the wall, exposing a narrow doorway. He took Elizabeth's hand and led her through it. They entered a room that was well-lighted and had five massive stone doors. Behind them, the opening closed as the bookcase returned to its original position. The room had a faint scent of lavender, calming and inviting.

Elizabeth looked around in wonder. Beautiful tapestries on each wall depicted scenes of dragons in various landscapes. The rugs were thick and decorated with dragons in flight, their scales seemingly alive with vibrant colors. Darcy watched her eyes devour everything; the room was a visual feast.

"Come, Elizabeth. We go downstairs to our quarters in the subterranean palace." He led her to a floor-to-ceiling tapestry on their right that covered the entrance to a stairway.

The temperature dropped slightly as they descended, the air carrying a faint hint of earthiness. The stone staircase spiraled down, their footsteps echoing softly against the walls. Elizabeth was excited to discover whatever lay below, the anticipation adding a sense of adventure to the moment.

The stairway ended in another circular room with three more massive stone doors. Darcy led her to the door on the left. The door had a magnificent carving of two dragons flying over a mountain, one gold and one white. He pressed his hand on the golden dragon. She watched as his hand changed into a clawed palm. Seconds later, it was only a hand again. The door opened. "Don't worry, my love. Kira will open the door for you, too. Your body will shift partially or fully when needed. Nobody enters our quarters uninvited."

Eyes wide, Elizabeth stared at the surroundings. Everything was ancient and beautiful. The scent of damp stone mixed with the earthy aroma of plants created an environment that felt natural and otherworldly. It was a massive cavern with a bathing pool the size of a grotto. The air was faintly humid, and the soft echoes of water droplets splashing into the pool added to the calming ambiance. The pool boasted a waterfall, the cascading water creating a soothing melody. There was a section with heated stones to rest upon, the warmth seeping through her skin as she approached. Plants and trees surrounded the pool, giving it a lush, verdant appearance. Openings in the stone walls hinted at more secluded areas beyond.

"Can you swim, Lizzy?" Darcy asked in a soft voice.

She nodded her head and walked towards the water. Darcy joined her, removing his clothes and tossing them aside as he walked. She blushed in embarrassment.

At the water's edge, he stood naked and gently pulled her close, silently undressed her, looking at her slender form, then took her hand and led her into the water.

"Let's swim, my love. I'll race you to the waterfall." The low baritone of Darcy's voice calmed her nerves.

She responded, "Fine, but I'm sure you will win..."

The water embraced her, its temperature perfectly balanced, creating a soothing sensation as she swam. She dove under the water, and the muffled sounds of the waterfall heightened the weightless feeling of being submerged. She rose to the surface. Her strokes were weak, propelling her slowly toward the goal.

Darcy awaited her behind the cascading water, standing on a small stone ledge, smiling. He helped her emerge from the water; the spray from the waterfall surrounded them, glistening droplets dancing in the air, covering them, sliding down their bodies, tracing paths along their skin as the natural setting heightened the experience.

He pulled Elizabeth close before lowering his head and gently kissing her lips. The taste of his kiss was a revelation, a sweet mingling of water and something uniquely him. It was her first kiss, and the sensation sent shivers down her spine. The air around them felt charged, and the embrace under the waterfall caused Elizabeth's body to respond to his kiss and touch with pleasure. Darcy deepened the kiss and began to stroke her body gently with his hands. He could feel her fear and her excitement.

He slowly released her lips and took her hand to pull her into the cave behind the waterfall. "Follow me, my love. It's time to give you a relaxing massage."

Still tingling from the kiss, Lizzy followed him through a passageway that opened into a massive room.

"Welcome to our suite, my love. I had it prepared with you in mind."

Speechless at the size of the room and awed by the opulent furnishings, Lizzy turned shocked eyes to her husband. The room seemed like a magical sanctuary, decorated with glowing crystals, flooding the space with ambient light. The play of light created a mesmerizing atmosphere, and the soothing sound of the waterfall outside provided a natural melody. The massive stone bed held several thick mattresses, soft pillows, and neatly folded quilted coverings, exuding an air of luxury. The stone side table had an array of bottles containing elixirs that promised indulgence. A choice of wine and liquor glasses sat on a nearby shelf.

Her husband's loving expression and the gentle glow of the ambient light added to the enchantment. Lizzy's eyes reflected surprise and gratitude as she took in the scene, silently acknowledging the effort he had put into creating a unique space for them. Lush rugs and tapestries added to the luxurious effect. The prisms casting rainbows across the room heightened the otherworldly atmosphere.

Caught in a moment of marvel, Lizzy realized that this underground retreat was more than a simple bedroom; it was a testament to Darcy's desire to provide her with an extraordinary life. She felt awe, gratitude, and appreciation for her husband.

With tenderness, Darcy picked her up and carried her to the bed. He placed Elizabeth on the soft mattress, turned her over, and with deliberate yet gentle movements, grasped a bottle of the lavender-scented oil, poured the liquid into his hands, and began spreading it over her back. The scent enveloped her, creating a sense of tranquility. Darcy kneaded her muscles expertly, and she felt the tension melting away under his skillful touch. Soon, he had her quivering from the intimate sensations of the massage.

Zander's venom, seeping from Darcy's pores, would enhance her pleasure, heal her, strengthen her body, and bind her to Darcy. His every touch elicited a moan of pleasure from Elizabeth's lips. He leaned in and kissed her neck while Zander directed the venom toward her pleasure center.

Darcy was concerned. Elizabeth's body was too thin, with lovely but small breasts, and her hips were too narrow for a grown woman. As he inspected his bride's form, his brow furrowed with worry.

Darcy voiced his concern to Zander, "Her body is underdeveloped. Consummating the bond will hurt her. I don't want to give her pain."

Zander replied, "Most female hosts are petite. The physical bonding must take place. Do not worry. Kira will help her body adapt to us. You have no choice."

"She is not petite, Zander. Something is wrong. Why can't Kira help before the consummation?"

"Kira says the girl will be fine. There is nothing to worry about. Concentrate on fulfilling your duty."

Elizabeth felt a fire growing inside her body. Every touch from Darcy fanned the flames. She was moaning in pleasure. When he began kissing her lips, she responded with wild passion. Her hands drew him closer, and her fingers ran through his thick, wavy hair. The feel of him against her skin was intoxicating.

Darcy deepened their kiss. Elizabeth responded by pulling him closer. Soon, their passion escalated until Elizabeth's pleasure peaked. When she calmed, Darcy started the process again. Her reactions were gratifying. He tried to put his fears aside and concentrate on giving her pleasure until her body was prepared for the next step. He continued to kiss and stroke her while whispering words of love, patiently waiting for his wife's body to adjust.

Zander, annoyed, growled in displeasure at the delay. "You must continue. Kira is adamant. Lizzy's body will adjust."

Zander released more venom, causing Elizabeth to writhe in pleasure, but Darcy sensed no change to her form and refused to comply.

Zander unsuccessfully tried to calm his host, "It will be fine. You must complete the bonding."

Darcy stroked his mate gently as he continued to whisper words of love to her, but he did not attempt to move.

Zander, impatient with Darcy, took control of his host and finished the process by releasing the bonding venom that would relax her muscles, enhance flexibility, promote healing, and bind her to Darcy alone.

Zander and Kira worked on healing Elizabeth while the couple slept.

Zander spoke, "They will be fine, won't they, Kira?"

Kira snapped, "Yes, she will love him deeply. Her eyes looked at him to seek his reactions every time he visited. Her youth confused his silence for indifference. Lack of experience confused her heart. She is no longer confused."

Zander was astounded. His queen avoided a direct answer. He bellowed, "I hurt her body. It scared and angered Darcy. He is furious that I forced the completion. She is so tiny inside. Her body is still growing. You hid the truth."

Kira answered flippantly, "It was unexpected. Her core was rigid. It resisted my attempts to make it expand. I had to enhance the growth of her pelvis. That is the reason the pain lasted so long. I've looked at her memories to determine the truth of her age. She is an adult."

"Darling, why do you keep trying to avoid the main issue? Why did you say the girl would be fine?"

Kira answered, "She remembers constantly being described as small for her age."

Zander roared, "A fourteen-year-old girl would have adapted quicker than Lizzy. Do you attempt to avoid taking responsibility for failing to fix the problem?"

Kira angrily responded, "Her body will be altered by Sunday night. I'm changing her bone structure with speed. At times, the accelerated growth may cause her pain. I will keep her unconscious. I suggest you do the same for Darcy since he becomes distressed when she feels even the slightest discomfort."

Zander, trying to be helpful, said, "Darcy has fallen asleep. I will ensure he does not wake up until you complete your task. Lizzy looks different already. Her breasts and hips are growing. The changes will please Darcy. Make sure she is uninjured. Let us pass the time until the changes are complete, singing our favorite songs."

Chapter 7

Darcy awoke for the first time in days. Lizzy was barely awake. "Come, my love, we need to bathe in the pool," Darcy whispered. Lizzy stared up at him but made no effort to rise.

"I feel strange," Lizzy muttered.

Darcy sat up. He pulled Elizabeth into his arms, stood quickly, and carried her to the water's edge, laughing aloud when he glanced at the waterfall. He gazed into her eyes with a mischievous smile and said, "Forgive me, my love. I can't resist." He tossed her through the air, and she landed in the pool directly beneath the waterfall.

Spitting water from her mouth, she rose under the cascade. Glaring at her husband, Elizabeth turned and swam to a small outcrop of land. She walked out of the water to stand on the tiny beach. Darcy followed her, appraising her dramatically changed body. Her hair was longer, she was taller, her muscles were toned, her abdomen was flat, her breasts were rounded, upright, and firm, and her hips were curvy. She had been beautiful before; now, she was magnificent.

At her inquisitive look, he spoke, "Lizzy, you're magnificent! Your body is perfect. I hope you like mine as much as I do yours."

Elizabeth studied the man standing next to her. She openly admired him with child-like innocence: his tall, muscular form, his attractive face, dark curly hair, and beautiful gray eyes that had specks of gold.

"Yes, William, I love your body very much. Come closer and kiss me, husband."

Darcy complied before dragging her into the water and splashing her with it. They played water games until hunger drove them ashore. He led the way to a small room where food waited on a low table, and thick body-length pillows served as seating. Darcy lay on his side, supporting his head with one hand and using the other to pluck food from the table and pop it into his mouth.

He watched Elizabeth attempt to get comfortable on a pillow on the opposite side of the table. He called out, "Come share my pillow. You are too far away. Let me feed you the tastiest morsels." He held out a small pastry to entice her.

In front of him sat a large goblet. It was full of a golden liquid. He added, "I know the perfect wine to excite your palate. It is called ambrosia. Nectar covers the sweets. You'll love their taste. Come join me, please."

Slowly, she made her way around the table, glancing at the items on it as she went to Darcy. She stood before him, and he reached for her hand to help her down. He held her close and arranged her legs for her. She looked uncomfortable but didn't complain.

"What troubles you, my heart? I want you to be comfortable in our home." His sincere words and concerned expression brought tears to her eyes.

"It's silly. I feel embarrassed that we're naked at dinner. It's strange to sit on pillows so close to the ground. I think I saw paintings of the Far East showing ancient times when people sat around tables like this. I can't remember. I'm being silly, just like Papa used to say." Elizabeth hung her head in embarrassment and looked at her hands.

Darcy sat up and pulled her into his arms. "We are bonded mates and do not need clothes in our private quarters. You feel different because intercourse with a dragon mate changes the female host's body. Your body adapted beautifully. It may take you a few days to get used to changes in your balance."

He kissed her passionately and palmed a breast. "Clothes are such an unnecessary barrier for this type of fun," he whispered into her ear, then gently sucked the sensitive spot at the base of her neck as his fingers pinched her nipple.

He murmured, "You are not silly, my love. We are all young once. Tutors will be hired to teach subjects that interest you and things you need to survive. Now we will eat and drink like Dionysus attending a picnic."

Darcy fed Lizzy various foods with one hand, continuously stroking her form with the other. She relaxed against his body, enjoying the meal and his touch. They drank prodigious amounts of ambrosia from the same golden goblet. There was a variety of meats and pieces of bread, including manna. Dessert consisted of spreadable jams, puddings, pastries, and a pot of warm melted chocolate to drip over the top of the delicacies.

The couple spent weeks alone in their cavern suite. Elizabeth learned to obey Darcy's instructions without question. He read to her, played games with her, engaged her in discussions, taught her to shift parts of her body, fed her, pleasured her body in countless ways, and taught her to do the same for him. Each day, he found time to train her in personal combat skills and the use of weapons.

Once Elizabeth could defend herself, they moved upstairs to the master suite in Darcy House. A modiste was called to the house, and measurements were taken. Styles and materials were ordered for a multitude of garments. Darcy stayed with her throughout the fittings, commenting on each design, fabric, and color.

When her new wardrobe arrived, Darcy accompanied her to their quarters, anxious to glimpse Elizabeth's reaction to each item. Dresses, cloaks, and undergarments littered the bed as Elizabeth unwrapped each parcel. The maids laughed with her as she held each gown up and exclaimed about the texture or style. Her surprised expression caused Darcy to laugh when she opened a large trunk containing slippers, walking shoes, boots, and other accessories to go with the dresses.

Darcy surveyed the rows of outfits lining the walls of her dressing room with a dissatisfied expression. "This is not enough. There is too much empty space here. We must fill it."

Taking Elizabeth by the hand, Darcy led the way to the entryway, calling for their outerwear and the carriage. Elizabeth gladly accompanied him to the shops, where more clothes and accessories were ordered. The experience made her feel like a princess from a fairytale, indulging in the luxury of choosing exquisite attire.

The following day, the knocker was placed on the front door, and visitors began to leave calling cards. Invitations to balls and other gatherings flooded in, creating a flurry of social activity. They selectively attended events hosted by close friends or family while politely declining others.

Elizabeth enjoyed dressing up for dinner with family and friends, visiting shops on Bond Street, and walking in Hyde Park. Darcy never left her side while she was awake. However, he had business concerns and used the predawn hours to perform his daily duties. Zander tasked Kira with keeping Elizabeth asleep during those times, especially if he had to be gone for more than three hours.

Chapter 8

Wednesday: November 15, 1809 - Darkness Discovered

Elizabeth awoke late one morning to discover Darcy wasn't home. Frantic, she asked Kira to find Darcy.

Kira scolded, "Relax. Darcy will be back by supper. An emergency in Norway required the king's presence. You are no longer a child. He cannot stay by your side every moment."

Elizabeth couldn't relax and went from room to room to distract herself, searching the shelves in the library for something to read. She grabbed a copy of Shakespeare's sonnets and opened it after sitting in her favorite armchair, but the words began to blur as her eyes filled with tears.

She closed the book and tossed it on the side table, pulling a handkerchief from her pocket to wipe her eyes. Lizzy was working herself into a hysterical state.

Kira grew concerned and took control of Lizzy; she walked the lady to the sofa and put her to sleep.

Kira delved into Lizzy's mind after deciding that something must be causing the girl to act irrationally and found a problem. There was a small pocket of darkness hidden in Elizabeth.

Darcy arrived late that night, tired and hungry. His frowning butler directed him to the library, where Elizabeth lay asleep on the sofa. Darcy rushed to Elizabeth and held her sleeping form in his arms.

Zander listened to Kira's story about the darkness hiding in Lizzy's mind, then relayed it to Darcy.

"Darcy, I will try to destroy the darkness. Carry her down to the palace caverns. I will need to take my form. Kira will open her eyes and steady her head as I search for evil. Someone has conspired against us in a most reprehensible manner."

Kira added, "This is a long-standing plot. I believe it is an attempt to corrupt my essence."

Zander gruffly responded, "You've been with her for weeks. You have grown lazy. You should have done better for your host than this."

Darcy picked up Elizabeth, carried her to the main cavern in the palace below, and went through the first door on the right, which opened into a circular vaulted chamber decorated with fine furnishings around a central area. He put her in a comfortable chair and moved away after stroking her cheek tenderly with his finger. He went to the cavern's center and became the golden dragon king.

Zander waited patiently for Kira to open Lizzy's eyes. His eyes glowed with dragon fire as he stared into her eyes, walked through the portal to her inner self, and searched her mind to find the tiny ball of darkness. It burnt into oblivion after being blasted with a spark of dragon fire. In its place, he left a small ball of light. Filled with love, kindness, and inner strength, the tiny ball expanded to fill the vacant spot. He continued to search through her memories. He didn't want to miss a single speck of dark magic. What he found was not darkness but excruciating pain.

When he finished the task, he placed a clawed hand on her head with enough pressure to pierce the skin. He injected healing venom directly into her skull. She had fallen down the stairs and suffered a severe concussion six years ago. He could feel the skull bone mending, a bone shard pushing upward through the skin. The shard was a tiny sliver, but it had put pressure on her brain. It had caused migraine headaches for two years until it shifted slightly and interfered with her hormone production. He sent more healing venom to hasten the process.

The king viewed memories of 'accidents' that mysteriously happened after arguments with her brother. He placed both claws over her abdomen. He sent wave after wave of healing venom into her reproductive system. He stood there all night fixing the internal damage caused when her ten-year-old brother stabbed her with a knife after a childhood argument over damage to a toy soldier. Her five-year-old self almost bled to death before her mother noticed the blood pouring from the wounds.

Zander spoke, "No wonder she isn't pregnant. Very thick scar tissue prevents her eggs from falling. The scar tissue is slowly dissolving; however, it will take days unless you take your proper form, Kira. There is room enough for both of us here. You must never join with a host in the future until we are sure she can reproduce and harbors no dark magic. Why didn't you tell me about the injuries this girl sustained in her childhood?"

Kira answered, "I've never searched for dark magic or childhood injuries in a potential host. It will be done on all potential candidates in the future. I didn't see any outward signs of lasting injury. When I did the earlier scan and found dark magic, I concentrated on removing it but couldn't. We are so old now. Sometimes I just want to sleep."

"You didn't check for problems during the bonding? You didn't investigate the cause behind her undeveloped structure?" growled Zander.

Kira sighed, "No, I did not. I'm sorry."

Zander snorted in anger. His mate was growing lazy.

Chapter 9

Friday: November 24, 1809 – Reflections

Darcy held his wife in his arms, waiting for her to wake. The damage to her body was completely healed. He hoped her mind would be strong enough to deal with the memories that Zander had to unlock while searching for any remaining speck of dark magic.

Zander said, "Kira apologizes for her failure. She begs your forgiveness."

Darcy angrily rejected Kira's apology. "Your negligence made Elizabeth's plight desperate. The healing could have taken place before the joining. Are you so tired of the world that you no longer care about the host you inhabit? You can hear me, Kira, even if you use Zander as an emissary. I know you can."

"I agree with Darcy. I'm sharing all the girl's memories with Darcy. How did you miss her pain?" asked the king. Kira didn't respond to them.

Darcy saw each of Elizabeth's *'accidents'* from her perspective. He experienced all the pain she felt throughout her life, including the pain inflicted by the bonding ritual. It had been excruciating for her. Her body was undeveloped. Lizzy had not grown due to the unseen damage. The bone splinter pressing into her brain that caused her migraines probably disrupted the process of growth. Kira had not noticed or cared.

Darcy kissed the top of Lizzy's head, holding his bride close. His enhanced senses could smell her pheromones and state of arousal. He had never detected the musky odor that indicated a fertile period.

Zander declared, "Our females do not have a monthly cycle like human women. Try to forgive Kira. This is the first time she has failed a host so severely."

Darcy stroked Elizabeth's cheek gently with a forefinger. She would wake soon, and her mind would be flooded with those horrifying memories.

"Kira, if you wish forgiveness, do not fail her when she wakes. She has suffered enough. I accept your apology but still hold you responsible for negligence. Zander is your heart. Elizabeth is mine."

He placed his chin atop Elizabeth's head and continued stroking her cheek with a finger. Darcy sighed. The waiting was difficult. Every few minutes, he kissed her hair. She had such beautiful dark, naturally wavy, auburn hair that she styled into charming ringlets. Her eyes were emerald with flecks of gold in their depths. When she lifted an eyebrow to express her indignation on a subject, it drove him mad with a desire to kiss her. His mate had to recover.

Time passed slowly for Darcy. The morning sun made its way west. Elizabeth stirred midafternoon. Her eyes slowly opened and met his. "Welcome back, my love. Can I get you something to eat or drink?" Darcy asked.

"I...think tea...maybe. I'm not...the library...what happened?" Elizabeth's eyes implored him to explain since she was confused.

Her countenance changed. Lizzy spoke her thoughts aloud, "How long did I sleep? Something is...missing? The aches...gone? How? Kira?!? Impossible...my brother? Not accidents? You did what? Zander took what out? Slow down...explain that...your fault? Now you help...now?" Suddenly, her eyes flashed a golden green, memories flooding her mind. A scream of agony pierced the air as her body shook in violent tremors.

Darcy held her close and whispered words of love into her ear. He begged her to remember only the good things from her past. Instead of tea, he gave her ambrosia to drink. "You survived it once; you can do it again for us. We are just starting our life together. Our love will create children to love. We will fly as dragons to far-off places and swim under the oceans. There is so much to see and do. Please think of happy things. You are my heart, Elizabeth. Stay with me," implored Darcy.

He pulled her closer and stroked her back. He plied her system with sips from goblets full of ambrosia and cakes covered in nectar to strengthen her body and mind. He wanted her to deal with the trauma without infusing her system with more venom.

"I love you, William. It is not your fault. Others are to blame. Do not fear for us. Promise to inform me before you go out without me...I was scared." Elizabeth spoke softly, but the words were clear.

Relieved that her sanity was intact, Darcy sighed softly, "Elizabeth, I love you, too. I will never leave on a trip without informing you in the future. I relied on another to tell you of my task when you woke. I hope you never have cause to fear for me again." His head bowed in sorrow.

"I let you down, Darcy. I should have taken more care to discover from Kira the reason Lizzy's body was so immature and in such pain. I am sorry for the pain I caused her to endure. She has an inner strength beyond my experience. She will recover. Will you?"

Darcy replied, "Yes. I will recover. You and I relied too much on your past experiences. We cannot leave her behind again. We must act on what we've learned from her memories."

"True. Now that we have a bonded mate, your identity as my host will become known. Extra care will be taken to protect both your bodies. I will create royal guard dogs with the general appearance of mastiffs[1] but armed with the height and claws of a massive lion in addition to the poisonous fangs of a serpent. The guard dogs will accompany her and stand watch whenever you call for them. They will be capable of understanding both mental and verbal commands from you and Elizabeth. I will call a conclave of the royals to act against the darkness. Those who created it will be purged from the planet. I will show no mercy."

---

1.   https://en.wikipedia.org/wiki/Mastiff

Chapter 10

Saturday: November 25, 1809

Darcy took Elizabeth to the underground palace accompanied by two guard dogs. They went through a door that led to the largest cavern. He took her to a suite adjoining it. "You'll be safe over here in this area, my love. This chaise is comfortable. Eat as much of the snacks on the tray as you like. I know you love to drink ambrosia. There is a small library further inside if you wish to read. Teach the dogs some new tricks." Darcy smiled at her when she kissed him on the cheek.

He continued, "I'll be transforming shortly and sit in the center of the large cavern. Bars will descend when I leave this space to keep you inside safely. If you get bored, try to nap on one of the mattresses you will find to your left." He pointed towards the bedding.

"This conclave will seek the source of the darkness that invaded your mind. Zander will be speaking with royals from all over the world. Kira will not take part. She needs to ensure your safety. That is the reason for the bars. Kira cannot be tempted to transform while those spreading darkness are eliminated. She would try to help Zander, and it is too soon to burden you with more painful memories," explained Darcy before pulling her into his arms and kissing her passionately.

He pulled away from her and left the cavern with a determined step. The bars descended, and Elizabeth watched as he went to the center of the large cavern and became Zander.

Zander turned toward Elizabeth and winked before settling down.

"Welcome, family. There is a problem. Darkness has begun to surface. Not at random but directed at harming my queen through my host's mate."

He incinerated close to a hundred kin when they tried to shut their minds to him.

"Sadly, we have just lost some of our numbers."

He felt their reactions to his words and incinerated over two hundred more royals.

"The death toll has risen to over three hundred."

He paused and waited.

"Good. We are down to the innocent or the exceedingly crafty ones."

He invaded their minds entirely without any warning, eliminating more royals.

"This has been a sad day for our family. To lose hundreds of my family to darkness is a tremendous sorrow. The rest of you will now begin searching for any remaining infected unclaimed hosts living in your area of the planet."

"I created this planet and every living thing, from the tiniest insect to the most enormous beast. I nurtured it for countless years. I am a creator. Other creators live out among the stars. We bring new life to the cosmos. We are not gods."

"Kira and I created billions of you over the eons. The hosts you take were created to serve as intelligent companions to conserve the planet's food supply. They eat less than our dragon form and are not to be used as weapons against us by humans practicing dark magic. Hosts have proven to be loyal, industrious, and creative. They are by far the most beloved of my creations besides my descendants. Darkness will never be allowed to destroy what has been built on this world."

"Perform your task. I'll seek the cause."

Ares spoke, "Father, how bad is the problem?"

Zander replied, "Worse than expected. People have been manipulated by human mages practicing dark magic into believing in gods and performing terrible acts. When you finish cleansing your lands, take flight and check the oceans and seas. Poseidon needs help."

He laid down with his head resting on a warm stone. Golden tears fell from his eyes. He had seen the mind that created this darkness. Minos, driven mad by a dark mage, believed himself a god and convinced his friends to follow him into the darkness. Incinerating a royal so ancient had caused tears. The death of James Bennet brought relief.

Hours later, the planet was searched four times. The last circuit was clear of darkness.

"We are done for today. Tomorrow, we'll deal with the aftermath."

Darcy gently stroked Elizabeth's cheek. His bride lay asleep on a pile of pillows, the loyal dogs nestled at her back, their warm bodies ensuring her comfort and safety. Her eyes fluttered open, and she sighed, stretching a leg and capturing his hand. "Is it done?" she asked softly.

"Yes," Darcy replied, his voice a soothing murmur. "The creators of the darkness, those spreading it, and those incurably infected by it are gone. Dealing with the world that survives is a problem for tomorrow. Tonight, we will rest."

Elizabeth smiled, a weary but relieved expression crossing her face. Darcy ordered the dogs away with a mental command, and they obediently retreated, settling nearby. He lay down beside his wife, pulling her into his arms. As he held her close, he felt the tension of the past hours begin to melt away.

"Thank you," she whispered, her voice barely audible.

"For what?" he asked, brushing a stray lock of hair from her forehead.

"For everything," she replied, her eyes closing again as sleep tried to reclaim her. "For being my strength, my protector, my love."

Darcy gently kissed her forehead, his heart swelling with affection. "Thank you for being my light in the darkness, Elizabeth."

As the chamber settled into a peaceful silence, the weight of their ordeals lifted, leaving only the comfort of each other's presence. Darcy tightened his embrace, and with a final, contented sigh, he allowed sleep to overtake him. They drifted into a deep, restorative sleep, their hearts beating in unison, ready to greet the dawn of a brighter tomorrow.

Chapter 11

<u>Monday: Scotland - December 25, 1809 – Christmas Day</u>

Four black horses pulled the large sled up the snow-covered driveway. It stopped under the covered porch that sheltered the carriage entrance of *Dragon's Deep Castle*. Darcy and Elizabeth disembarked and ran to the door that swung open at their approach. Footmen followed the couple carrying armloads of packages, closely followed by four large guard dogs.

Laughter filled the hallway as Darcy and Elizabeth shed the snow-covered outerwear that did not keep the falling white flakes at bay. "You look like a tall snowman, William," Elizabeth called out as she tried to stifle her giggles.

"Well, you are a beautiful little snow lady!" Darcy responded with a chuckle and a wide smile. He added, "I didn't realize a storm was coming or people would keep tossing snowballs at us when we stopped to greet them."

"And all these packages you hid in the rectory! We must give them out after breakfast." Elizabeth was amazed that Darcy hid so many personal gifts for the household staff's children in the village rectory. He explained that it was a tradition to hide gifts in different locations yearly because the staff had numerous children who searched the castle to find them before Christmas.

The packages contained dolls, toy soldiers, kites, model boats, ice skates, sleds, paints, sketch pads, canvases, balls, and other items the children wanted. This year, Elizabeth helped him pick out the items from a list supplied by the housekeeper while shopping in town. Watching the children open the presents would be a joyful experience.

After going to their suite to warm up by the fire and change into dry clothes, Elizabeth and Darcy descended the grand staircase, their fingers intertwined. The warmth of the fire had chased away the chill, and Elizabeth felt a renewed sense of comfort as they made their way to the dining room. There, the delightful hum of conversation greeted them, and Elizabeth's heart swelled with happiness.

Breakfast was a merry affair. Elizabeth exchanged smiles and laughter with her family, her spirits lifted by the sight of her sisters and the Gardiners at the table. Once everyone had eaten their fill, they moved to the ballroom, a grand space decorated with colorful ribbons, holly, mistletoe, and wreaths for the festive occasion. In the center of the room stood a table piled high with colorfully wrapped parcels, each bearing a name tag attached to its ribbon.

Darcy took his place behind the table with Elizabeth at his side. He glanced at her with a warm smile before addressing the gathering. "We have some gifts for the children. Let's make this a joyous occasion for them."

Elizabeth nodded, her eyes sparkling with excitement. "Yes, let's."

The children entered through the door, the youngest leading the line, their eyes wide with anticipation. Each child approached the couple, offering a shy thank you before eagerly running off to find a spot to open their gift. Elizabeth's heart melted at their joy, and she shared a tender look with Darcy.

As the children tore into their parcels, their delighted squeals filled the room. The adults watched with fond smiles, and Elizabeth felt a deep contentment. When the last gift had been unwrapped, the footmen efficiently moved the table to the wall closest to the doorway.

Within minutes, servants bearing refreshments appeared, covering the table with platters of candies, cakes, and an array of sweet treats on one side while the other offered a selection of meats, cheeses, and bread. Another table held bowls of fruit punch for the youngsters, tureens of hot beverages, and decanters of port and whiskey. A sideboard nearby was laden with crockery of all types.

Elizabeth turned to Darcy, a soft smile on her lips. "Everything looks wonderful. You've truly outdone yourself." Her husband insisted on planning this event, claiming it was a tradition.

Darcy chuckled, placing a gentle hand on her back. "I couldn't have done it without you."

An impromptu concert by the family soon followed, their harmonious voices filling the ballroom. The music paused only when the professional musicians finished setting up near the floor-to-ceiling windows on an elevated platform. As the first lively notes of a jig filled the air, Darcy extended his hand to Elizabeth.

"Shall we dance, Mrs. Darcy?"

Elizabeth laughed, her eyes twinkling. "I thought you'd never ask, Mr. Darcy."

They led the first dance, their movements graceful and in sync. Couples joined them, and soon, the ballroom was alive with dancing. Tenants and staff drifted in and out throughout the day, partaking in the festivities. The food and drinks were constantly replenished, ensuring everyone remained well-fed and merry.

The musicians played in rotation, their brief breaks allowing new groups of performers to take the stage. The continuous music kept the energy high, and everyone, including the children, danced. Elizabeth watched with delight as the little ones twirled and stepped, supervised by their parents and older siblings.

As the day wore on, Elizabeth found herself in Darcy's arms again, the room spinning with joy around them. She looked up at him, her heart full. "This is perfect, Darcy. Truly perfect."

Darcy leaned down, brushing a kiss against her forehead. "It's perfect because you're here, Elizabeth. You make everything brighter."

Elizabeth's smile widened, and she nestled closer to him, the warmth of his embrace matching the warmth in her heart. Together, they continued to dance, the world outside forgotten as they celebrated the start of their new life together.

By the end of the night, Elizabeth was exhausted. She fell into bed with a giant smile on her face. It had been such a delightful day. Darcy joined her under the covers and pulled her into his arms. "Did you have fun, my love?"

Elizabeth sighed happily, "Oh yes! It was the best day ever!" She snuggled closer to his side and looked up into his golden gray eyes with a mischievous smile on her lips. "Did you ever find your present?"

"Of course, I found you when I opened my eyes! You're the best present, my dear," he replied, kissing her gently. Elizabeth returned his kiss and tousled his hair.

She stretched her arm until her fingers grasped a velvet box under her pillow. Nervously, she held it out to Darcy.

"This is for you, William. It's just a little trinket. I hope you like it." Her green eyes watched him take the box and slowly open it. His face lit up with pleasure, and she was content. It was a thin golden case that opened on a delicate hinge. The outside was plain, but the inside featured engraved portraits of Darcy and Elizabeth facing each other with the words:

Two hearts Are one. Locked Together Forever In Love.

The back of the case had an etched heart with their wedding date inscribed. The case would easily fit into the inner pocket of a vest or jacket. Darcy was touched by the thoughtfulness of this remarkable young woman who showed her love for him in surprising ways every day.

"It is a most thoughtful gift. I will always carry it with me, Lizzy. Thank you for creating this amazing work of art. Did you do the lettering, too?"

She answered him softly, "I'm happy you like it. I practiced engraving on sheets of gold the jeweler sold to me. He assured me the sheets could be melted down to create something else later." With a teasing laugh, she added, "Getting the details of your hair was the hardest part."

Elizabeth wrapped her arms around his waist to snuggle closer to his side and closed her eyes in contentment. "I'm glad you fell in love with me, William. You, Zander, and Kira saved me in so many ways. I love you dearly."

Darcy looked at her to drink in her beauty. His heart knew her as his mate the instant she walked into the parlor at Rosings to be introduced to his aunt. He began writing love letters to her that night in a journal. Every day, he found time to write to her of his love. His heart had never been mistaken.

This morning, he had wrapped the journal in a silver cloth and secured it with a red ribbon tied in a big bow. A red rose from the hothouse was placed beside it on her dressing table. When Elizabeth found it there, she smiled. The sweet, happy smile she wore was replaced with a joyful one as she read each entry. Watching her read the letters was a gift few men would ever experience with their wives. Her face reflected her thoughts. He knew that Elizabeth's heart was mistaken no more.

The End

Author's Note

Here are a few images for you.

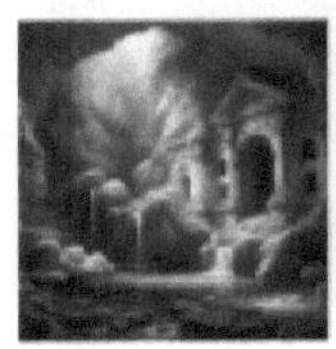

Thank You!

Reviews help authors more than you might think.
If you enjoyed this story, please leave a positive review.

Did you love *Mistaken Heart*? Then you should read *Born to Serve*[1] by Linda Wagner!

[2]

Warning: Mature Audiences Only. Some content may trigger adverse reactions in sensitive individuals.

Immerse yourself in a unique blend of dark paranormal fantasy and the timeless world of Pride and Prejudice. In this dragon-themed saga, Zander and Kira, soulmates who birthed a galaxy, have made Earth their primary masterpiece. Their extraordinary bond and powers are central to the story.

Darcy and Elizabeth are hosts to these immortal dragon spirits. They navigate a realm where the dragon king and queen reign over an entire galaxy. This fantastical world, while reminiscent of Regency England, is brimming with magical and social differences.

---

1. https://books2read.com/u/3117Bv

2. https://books2read.com/u/3117Bv

In this tale of love and pride, Darcy is deeply in love with Elizabeth and fully aware of his dragon host status. Elizabeth, however, remains ignorant of her own, her dragon's voice mysteriously silent. Darcy's passionate proposal offends Elizabeth's pride, revealing his meddling in Jane Bennet's romance with Charles Bingley, leading to a stunning revelation.

Will Elizabeth overcome her pride and accept Darcy's proposal? Will dark magic complicate their future? Will the schemes of hostile relatives overshadow their happiness?

Filled with suspense, unexpected twists, and mature themes, this dark fantasy reimagines familiar characters in a new light, diverging from Austen's originals. It promises readers an unpredictable adventure as Darcy and Elizabeth pursue their happily ever after.

Approximately 121,000 words

Also by Linda Wagner

Darcy & Elizabeth: Finding Love
Practice Makes Perfect

Dragons, Deceit, and Desire
Born to Serve
Mistaken Heart

Short Stories
Dancing With Pistols
The Right Choice

Standalone
Jane: A Born to Serve Bonus Chapter
Dark Before Light

About the Author

L. Wagner lives in Texas and is happily married to a wonderful man who indulges their cat with daily treats. She enjoys writing as a hobby and enjoys reading Pride and Prejudice variations, mysteries, paranormal fantasy, and science fiction.

A Pride and Prejudice fan since the 1960s, she finally decided to contribute a few stories to the JAFF community. Hopefully, the twists and turns of her imagination will interest you.

www.ingramcontent.com/pod-product-compliance
Lightning Source LLC
Chambersburg PA
CBHW051807130726
47987CB00003B/1151